When is it Going to Rain?

gina sano

To order additional copies of this book, contact:
Xlibris
AU TFN: 1 800 844 927 (Toll Free inside Australia)
AU Local: 0283 108 187 (+61 2 8310 8187 from outside Australia)
www.xlibris.com.au
Orders@Xlibris.com.au

ISBN: Softcover   978-1-5245-2195-0
        Hardcover   978-1-5245-2197-4
        EBook   978-1-5245-2196-7

Print information available on the last page.

Rev. date: 07/18/2017

When is it Going to Rain?

gina sano

It has been hot and dry for a very long time. Mum and dad said this was the worst drought for a very long time. I wondered when it was going to rain.

I asked my grandma, "When is it going to rain?"

She gave me a smile and said, "I know when it is going to rain. My knees ache. But it is not going to rain today or tomorrow."

So I asked my granddad, "When is it going to rain?"

Granddad smiled as he stretched his back. He said, "I know when it is going to rain. My back aches. But is not going to rain today or tomorrow."

Mum was sweeping the floor when I asked her, "When is it going to rain?"
She looked up and wiped a sweaty brow. "I know when it is going to rain. Ants invade the kitchen. There are no ants in the kitchen. I think they are hiding outside. It is not going to rain today or tomorrow."

I ran outside to find some ants. It took me a long time but I found some under a few dead leaves at the bottom of the orange tree. I was trying not to disturb the ants but they started to run around fast. Some stood up on their back legs as if they were trying to talk to me. I am sure they said, "We know when it is going to rain. You humans keep looking at us. Do you know when it is going to rain?" "No." I whispered and walked away.

I went to the back of the house where my pet dog was sleeping in his bed. "Rusty," I asked, "do you know when it is going to rain?"

He looked at me with is his big brown eyes and rolled over on to his back. He nudged his nose on my hand. This was his way of saying, "Pat me."

Then, I remembered Dad saying Rusty sleeps on his back and his paws are in the air a day before the rain. No rain; Rusty was sleeping on his tummy.

"It is not going to rain today or tomorrow," I whispered.

Then I remembered Mrs. Smith, the lady who lives next door once told me about her cat. "Madam," Mrs Smith said, "sleeps on her back with her paws in the air a day before the rain.
I pushed my face up against the gap in the wooden fence to see where Madam was. I saw her in the shade under Mrs. Smith's steps and she was sleeping the right way on her tummy.
It is not going to rain today or tomorrow, I thought.

Mr. Brown, who lives across the road, used to be a farmer. He told me stories about the farm and the animals. He always said, "The crows would fly close to the ground or even walk on the ground just before the rain."

I looked at the sky and at Mr. Brown's tall gum tree in his back yard. There was not a bird in sight.

It is not going to rain today or tomorrow, I thought.

My Uncle Ben came over with my cousin Brad. My Uncle Ben likes to feed birds in his
backyard. *I will ask him*, I thought, *if he knows when it is going to rain*.
Uncle Ben gave me a cuddle and placed me on his knee. He poured me a glass of water from the big
jug in the middle of the table. "I know when it is going to rain, because a peewee comes to my front
glass door and taps it until I answer. He hasn't come to the door at all so it is not going to rain today
or tomorrow."

I noticed that Brad had a silly grin on his face. He said, "Everyone be quiet for a moment and listen!"
Everyone was quite; not a sound was heard.

 "There," said Brad, "Did you hear that?"
We all shook our heads.

"Exactly! That's it!" Brad said with a smile on his face, "There are no crickets or frogs. Neither is making a noise. It is not going to rain today or tomorrow."

Later that night, I was sitting on the veranda beside Brad. I told him of all the different ways people told me they knew it was going to rain.

He looked up at the moon and said (with that same silly grin on his face), "There was one more way."

"What?" I asked. "Another way?"

He nodded and then pointed to the moon. "This is something I learned by myself, and most times it is right. What do you see around the moon?"

"Nothing. It is shining bright. There are a few stars."

"Yes. You're right. Every night take a look at the moon. When you see rings around the moon, that means it *could* rain. When the rings go closer and closer to the moon, that means rain is on the way."

"Oh," I said as I looked at the moon again, trying to see some rings. Then I said softly, "It's not going to rain tonight or tomorrow."

Weeks went by as I watched for the signs of rain. Just when I was thinking it was never going to rain again, things began to change. One night, the moon had a yellowish ring around it! Each night, the ring went closer and closer and became brighter and brighter.

Rain is on the way, I thought.

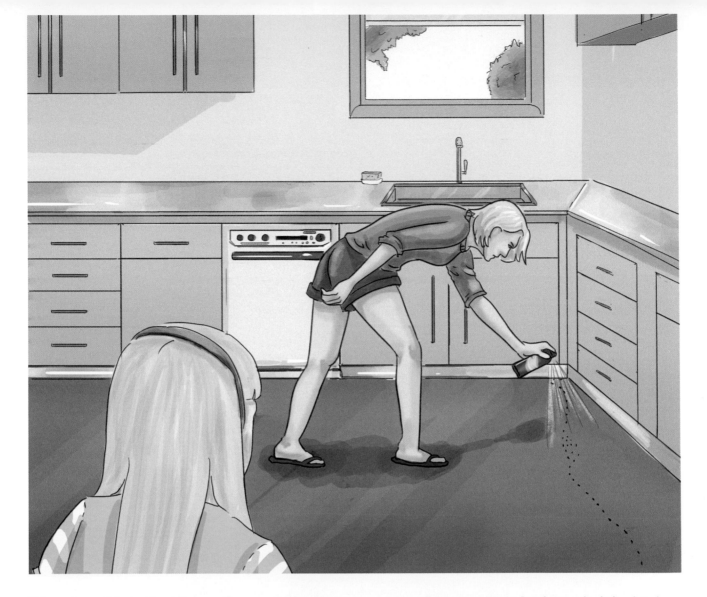

When I went into the kitchen the next day, Mum was using the spray. Ants had invaded the kitchen and other parts of the house. She said, "Stay back from the spray. See all the ants? It is going to rain *maybe* later today or tomorrow."

14

I ran to the back door and saw Rusty sleeping on his back and his paws in the air. I tried to slip past him but he rolled over and followed me. I peered through the gaps in the timber fence, and I saw Madam sleeping on the bottom of Mrs, Smith's steps. She was also on her back with her paws in the air. She rolled over quickly when she heard Rusty give a growl.

It's going to rain today or tomorrow, I thought.

I went to the orange tree to where I saw the ants a long time ago. They were very, very busy carrying things into their nest.

I looked away from the nest when I noticed loud noises.

That must be crickets and frogs, I thought.

"It is going to rain today or tomorrow," I whispered back to ants.

I went inside to see if Grandma and Granddad were up. Grandma was sitting on a chair and rubbing her knees. Grandad talking on the phone to Uncle Ben.

I heard granddad complain to Uncle Ben about his aching back. When grandad finished his call, he turned to grandma and said, "Ben has the peewee making a mess at his front door."

"Ah!" I said to grandma and to granddad as I watched them rub their aches and pains. "Rain is on the way!"

From my bedroom window I looked at the sky for birds. Crows were flying close to the ground and sometimes chasing other birds away.

Yes, I thought. *It is going to rain - and it's going to today.*

Later that day dark grey clouds filled the eastern sky and the temperature started to drop. Then I heard pitter-patter as rain drops fell softly. At first it was quiet and gentle but the more it rained, the louder, faster and heavier it became. It rained all day and most of the night.

The next day the sky was blue and everything smelled fresh and clean. Now I know when it will rain and I am am the only one who knows everyone's secret. Now I know when it is going to rain.

Other books in print by Gina Sano:
Follow the Leader.